ROSETHORN ACADEMY

Laura Shenton

ROSETHORN ACADEMY

Laura Shenton

Iridescent Toad Publishing

Iridescent Toad Publishing.

Cover by RJ Creatives.

First edition. ISBN: 978-1-913779-42-9

Chapter One

Talia had always believed in magic. Whenever she flew through the dense forests of Calyun, her acutely-angled dark-tipped wings beating rapidly and her long raven hair billowing like a veil, she couldn't help but feel a sense of wonder at the world around her. The way the sunlight filtered through the leaves, the way the flowers bloomed, and the way the wildlife moved – all of it felt as though it was infused with a beautiful, mystical energy.

Having always lived with her parents on their farm, Talia spent her days tending to the plants and animals, but her true passion was for the magic that she believed lay just beyond the edges of her reality.

None of the other fae in Calyun shared Talia's enthusiasm for magic. All of them, including her parents, thought it was a stupid and dangerous idea. They would often tell her that only reckless fae chose to mess with magic.

Although Talia had never dared to engage with any magic, her desire to explore it was always at the front of her mind. She had every faith that it could be used for good, convinced that it could transform a patch of barren ground into a lush meadow, or make a river flow in the opposite direction. In her frustration that everyone around her was so closed-minded, she would often question them about it.

"How can you be so against magic if you've never even tried it?" she asked her father one day as they were feeding their chickens.

"There's no need for it," Droylsden said with a grunt as he bent down to scatter the feed with labour-calloused hands, his grey wings catching the light as he moved.

"You can't be certain of that," she said.

Talia's mother – Sarelda – let out a deep sigh. Tucking a strand of long mousey-brown hair behind her ear, she then moved to place a gentle hand on her daughter's shoulder.

"We've discussed this numerous times already," Sarelda said. "Must we go through it again?"

"Yes!" Talia insisted. "We've gone through this time and time again, and nobody has ever given me a straightforward response. I don't believe you have one either! There's no justification for being so against the use of magic when it could turn out to be helpful for us!"

"All we ask is that you stay away from magic," Sarelda said quietly, her tawny-coloured wings twitching with displeasure.

Annoyed, Talia violently hurled a handful of seeds at the ground, startling a cluster of gathered chickens.

"What if I don't want to?" she asked, struggling to temper her exasperation. "What if I want to go to the academy in Priggly?"

With expressions of shock and dismay, Talia's parents glared at her, evidently offended.

"Talia!" Sarelda asserted, using her tone to caution her daughter.

"You mean Rosethorn Academy!?" Droylsden asked, his voice rising in anger. "That establishment is intended for ignorant fae who have nowhere else to turn! It's a place for the troublemakers of this world to seek comfort amongst the taboo. Rosethorn Academy is not for respectable fae! No, Talia. Don't ever bring this up again!"

With a sigh, Talia cast her gaze down at the chickens, sadly watching as they pecked hungrily at the dry ground.

"Your father simply wants what is best for you," Sarelda offered, eager to console her daughter and ease the tension in the air. "And so do I."

"How can you be certain of what's best for me?" Talia debated. "I'm an adult, Mother. Eventually, you will have to let me make my own choices."

"I know," Sarelda replied sorrowfully, her countenance reflecting surrender. "But when it comes to something like Rosethorn

Academy, it's not your decision to make. That terrible place is out of the question. Besides, your father and I have been discussing the idea of granting you some land. You could establish your own farm on it, and if you were to marry soon..."

"Mother, I can't!" Talia interjected sharply, causing her mother to fall silent. "I can't simply get married and start a farm. I can't follow in your footsteps! I'm glad you're both happy with your chosen path in life, but that's not what I want, and it never will be! I know you mean well, but all the same..."

"Talia, please," Sarelda implored. "Don't push us away like this. We only want..."

"Mother, have you ever considered that Rosethorn Academy might be what's best for me?"

Sarelda exhaled heavily, bringing the conversation to a standstill.

Talia dropped her bag of feed, the contents scattering on the ground.

"I need to take a break," she said. "I need to clear my head."

Leaving her parents with the chickens, she stormed off to be on her own, her steps heavy with indignation. As the golden hues of the wheat fields slowly dissolved behind her, she ruminated on how the argument was not a new one. She had been engaging in the same dispute with her parents since turning eighteen. At odds with their aspirations of wanting her to establish herself as a farmer, she yearned for the freedom to explore her passion for magic. Her parents' vision of what her life should be, although respectable and safe, was too predictable, too boring.

Just as she had done many times before, Talia walked the full length of Calyun, tracing the river's edge, looping back through the forest, passing by the village square, and eventually heading back towards her parents' farm where she had spent the past twenty-two years. The walks granted her a rare sense of freedom, where she could be herself without apology, unburdened by the expectations of others. They served to provide a safe haven where she could look at the flowers around her and wonder about the possibilities for magic without fear of judgment.

"It's maddening how closed-minded they

are," she said to herself. "They can't even entertain the idea that they might be mistaken. They don't have any evidence or logical reasoning. How can they expect me to simply agree with them?"

As her temper flared, with a swift kick, she sent a nearby stone, small and jagged, skittering across the ground, a physical release for the pent-up emotions swirling within her. Yet, as the stone slowed to a halt, so did her outward display of anger, giving way to a deep, melancholic pause.

"I'm stuck in the same old cycle," she confided to the wind, which whistled through the trees. "Maybe if there were other options or things to focus on, it wouldn't be so bad. As beautiful as Calyun may be, there's nothing here for me – just farming as I long for something more."

She let out a soft sigh, but suddenly became silent as she noticed the presence of something marvellous: one of the most taboo flowers of all.

A rose.

Chapter Two

Talia had seen roses before, but they were a rare sight in Calyun. The magic-fearing fae would always destroy them at the earliest sign of a new bloom.

Mesmerised by its very presence, she knelt beside the rose, studying it from every angle, trying to absorb every detail of its exquisite form. Its petals were a deep shade of crimson. The stem was sturdy and strong, yet graceful in the way it arched towards the sky.

She reached out to touch the curve of a petal, enchanted by its velvety softness against her fingertips. She marvelled at the way it seemed to shimmer in the sunlight.

For several minutes, she allowed herself to become lost in the wonder of the rose's beauty. It was as though time had stopped, and all that existed in the world was her and the single flower.

It's incredible. If only I could embrace its magic without having to fear the consequences.

Hearing the sound of young fae playing nearby, Talia quickly got up and took a step back from the rose. Everyone in Calyun knew that she had always been so curious about magic; she didn't want to draw attention to herself, or the rose, which would surely result in it being promptly destroyed.

Before turning to walk away, she looked at the rose longingly. It made her sad to think of how someone would eventually find it and cut it down without a second thought.

I've had enough. I just can't do this anymore.

To remain in Calyun would stifle her. Deep down, Talia knew that there had to be more to life, and more to the magic that she yearned to understand.

If I could just go to Rosethorn Academy, I could learn all about the magic of a rose's thorns. I believe so deeply that there is no evil to magic, and that good could come from having the skills to get the best out of nature. How can something that's all around us be as awful as some of the fae in Calyun like to insist? I would be responsible and careful in my approach to magic. I just feel so ready to embrace it.

Talia had contemplated leaving for Rosethorn Academy on numerous occasions, but had never advanced to the stage of taking action.

Maybe it's time.

Confronting her true feelings, she acknowledged that her only reluctance to attend the academy was due to fear. If she were to leave the village for the academy, her parents would most likely disown her. She would lose everything she had ever known and would have to build a new life from scratch. Consequently, a faint trail of uncertainty lingered, pestering her with questions.

What if the academy's not all it's cracked up to be? What if I fail? I couldn't show my face around here again.

Overall, unable to rid her mind of the beautiful rose she had just seen, Talia was certain of her desire to go to Rosethorn Academy. She couldn't stand the thought of giving in to her parents and quietly accepting the farming life that she desperately didn't want.

Perhaps the only thing that's truly stopping me is myself. Perhaps it's time to be brave.

Chapter Three

As the fading light of the setting sun bathed the room in a soft golden glow, Talia sat at the table with her parents. Meticulously set, porcelain plates hand-painted with intricate patterns gleamed in the low light. Each utensil had been placed with care, testament to the thought with which the meal had been prepared. At the centre of the table was a simple wooden bowl overflowing with freshly-picked berries. Each one, plump and succulent, glistened with the dew of the early evening, serving as a reminder of the earth's bounty. Next to the bowl of berries lay a loaf of rustic bread, still warm from the oven, its tantalising scent filling the air. Accompanying the bread and berries were small bowls of honey and nuts.

"Can you pass the salt, please, Talia?" Sarelda asked.

Without making eye contact, Talia complied with the request.

I need to tell them I'm leaving.

"I think some flowers are starting to come through out in the field," Talia's father said to her mother. "I'll tear up the ground again tomorrow, just to be sure that nothing untoward gets through."

"That's good," said Sarelda. "It's better to be safe than sorry."

"Indeed," said Droylsden.

Sarelda noticed her daughter's annoyance, but decided to disregard it, instead directing her attention to her husband to continue their conversation.

"Do you think we're safe here, Droylsden?" she asked.

"I believe so, my love," he responded. "It's been a very long time since there was last an attack on the village. As long as we do everything we can to keep any fragment of potential magic at bay, we should be alright."

"Perhaps magic is only dangerous in the wrong hands," Talia spoke up, her tone laced with defiance.

"Excuse me?!" her father demanded.

Say it!

Talia inhaled deeply.

"I've made up my mind," she declared. "I'm going to Rosethorn Academy."

Sarelda's movements halted abruptly as if time itself had paused, her expression one of shock and fear. Droylsden's features contorted into a deep scowl, his brow furrowed with displeasure.

"No, you're not," he said bluntly, his anger simmering beneath.

"I am," Talia insisted, shaking a little, but resolute.

"You are not!" he exclaimed, raising his voice. "We've had this discussion before. Rosethorn Academy is meant for uneducated lowlifes who have no other option! They take in lost and confused fae who are naive and easily persuaded. Rosethorn Ac..."

"Blah, blah, blah!" Talia interjected, her voice rising to match her father's. "How can you say that when you haven't even been there?!"

"Don't you dare raise your voice at me, young lady!"

"You never listen, so now, *I'm* going to stop listening. I'll pack my belongings and leave at dawn," Talia said, feeling certain about her plan.

"If you do that, don't ever come home again," her father said plainly.

"Fine," Talia snapped back, already striding towards her bedroom.

She swiftly began packing her belongings into a leather satchel. She wouldn't need to take much with her – just a few changes of clothes and footwear, one of her cherished books, and some provisions for survival. The sound of her parents quarrelling downstairs made her feel remorseful, particularly when she heard her mother sobbing. She had to firmly remind herself that having come this far, she couldn't back down.

If I change my mind now, I'll be stuck here forever. If I don't leave immediately, I'll never have the bravery to do so.

Just as she had finished packing, Talia heard a knock at her bedroom door. When she opened it, she discovered her mother standing there, her eyes brimming with tears and her lips trembling.

"Please stay, Talia," Sarelda urged. "Your father is against you leaving. If you do, he'll cut ties with you. I can't bear the thought of never seeing you again."

As she broke down into a fresh wave of tears, Sarelda reached out and held her daughter tightly. With a deep sadness in her heart, Talia welcomed her mother's embrace, knowing that it was probably the last time they would be able to hold each other. Finally though, she pulled away, pained, but more determined than ever.

"Please, Talia, reconsider," Sarelda begged, her voice barely audible as she gazed into her daughter's eyes with desperation.

"I'm sorry," said Talia, "but I have to go."

"I don't understand," Sarelda said weakly.

"I know," said Talia, acknowledging her mother's predicament with sympathy. "Neither of you can comprehend my fascination with magic. I need to be around fae who can."

Now determined not to delay her journey until the morning, Talia picked up her bag and bypassed her mother. She headed straight to the kitchen, where she quickly filled a flask with water and stashed it away.

Her father stood there glaring at her.

"May I take some food with me?" she asked.

"Droylsden, do something!" Sarelda called out.

"Take some bread," he said flatly.

Determined to maintain her composure and behave with grace, Talia thanked him and then carefully took a modest amount of food from the table, packing it in her bag with the rest of her supplies.

"Mother, Father, I bid you farewell," she said gently. "May you both be happy and safe. Look after each other."

Droylsden comforted Sarelda by putting his arm around her as she continued to cry. A fury remained in his eyes as he stood defeated and resigned.

"I hope your journey brings you the answers you seek, Talia," he said pragmatically.

Certain that she was making the right decision, and ready to embrace whatever her new life would bring, Talia stepped outside and gently shut the front door behind her.

Chapter Four

With the route being long and unfamiliar, and considering the weight of her bag, Talia had chosen to walk rather than fly. On her way out of Calyun, at the spot where she had seen the rose, she had paused briefly to see if it was still there. Saddened to see that it wasn't, and assuming that it had been destroyed, she resumed her journey along the path towards the next village. Despite the pain in her legs, she had her sights firmly set on the town of Priggly, the home of Rosethorn Academy.

As the sun emerged with the light of a new dawn, Talia was sore, exhausted and hungry. She continued to walk until she came across a large rock to rest upon. Gratefully sitting down to take a break, she hungrily ate some of the bread she had packed. Then, despite her muscles aching in protest, she soon settled into a steady pace as she got moving again.

She anticipated that if she continued to keep good time, she would arrive at the academy the following day. She couldn't help but feel proud of herself for what she had already accomplished, believing that it would surely bode well for her newfound independence.

She continued to walk for most of the day, until finally, she could see the town of Priggly on the horizon like a shimmering oasis, its charming silhouette bathed in the warm hues of the late-afternoon sun. Clusters of quaint cottages adorned with colourful blooms dotted the landscape, their roofs peeking out amidst a sea of lush greenery. The gentle breeze carried with it the sweet scent of wildflowers. The town square bustled with life as fae flitted about, going about their routines with a sense of purpose and contentment. Vibrant market stalls lined the cobblestone streets, offering an array of fresh produce and artisan crafts that spoke of the town's thriving community spirit.

As Talia took in the sight of Priggly, a realisation slowly began to dawn upon her:

this place was far grander and more active than her quiet village back home. She had never known anywhere other than Calyun. It was at this point that the enormity of the situation caught up with her. She wondered if it was possible to simply walk into the academy, or if there was an application process that needed to be followed before admission could be granted. Despite how much she had been thinking about going there, her knowledge of it was based solely on hearsay and rumours.

There's so much that I don't know.

Despite her anxieties, Talia reminded herself to remain calm and to approach the situation one step at a time. Aware that the sun was beginning to set, she noted that her first priority should be to find a suitable place to spend the night. After a good night's rest, she would be able to plan ahead in the morning.

As her tired feet continued along the cobblestones, she decided to try the first tavern in sight – The Enchanted Acorn. Its welcoming exterior, adorned with twinkling lights and blooming flower boxes, beckoned her to step inside. As she pushed open the heavy wooden door, she was greeted by the comforting glow of lanterns casting dancing shadows upon the polished oak floors. Cosy and inviting, plush velvet cushions lined the surrounding wooden benches, whilst a crackling fireplace provided a gentle warmth throughout the room.

The establishment was lively, teeming with patrons who were all engaged in animated conversations and laughter. At the bar, fae served up frothy mugs of honeyed ale and glasses of sparkling nectar with a friendly smile. From the looks of it, the tavern was quite unlike the quieter spaces that Talia had become so used to back in Calyun.

More impressed by her surroundings than daunted, she walked up to the bar.

"How much would it cost for a room for the night?" she asked the bartender.

"A private room will cost you ten coins. A shared room is five," he replied as he continued to polish a glass with a cloth. "A shared room comes with two single beds."

With little money in her possession, Talia

knew that she needed to be mindful of her expenses. However, she was worried about the possibility of being paired with someone unpleasant.

"Who would I be sharing a room with?" she asked.

The bartender gestured towards a young woman who was seated at a table by the window. Relaxed in her demeanour, she was eating a sandwich.

"She has requested a shared room," he said. "Perhaps you would like to share with her."

"Thank you," said Talia. "I'll go and ask her if she wants to share with me."

"Sure. Let me know what you decide," the bartender said as he turned to address another customer's order.

Taking a deep breath, Talia approached the young woman. Like Talia, she seemed to be in her early twenties. She had long silver hair and serene blue eyes. Her wings were a dark-grey colour with pink detailing around the edges.

"Hey there," said Talia.

"Hi," the young woman responded cheerfully as she paused her meal.

"Just to let you know," said Talia, "I would be happy to share a room with you. I've had a long journey and I only wish to sleep."

"That works for me," said the woman. "Do you want to get something to eat? I'll treat you."

"That's very kind of you," Talia said, surprised by the offer as she took a seat at the table. "Are you sure?"

"Absolutely!" said the woman. "I really appreciate that you'll be sharing the cost of a room with me. Oh, and by the way, my name's Periwinkle, but everyone calls me Perin. What's your name?"

Perin waved enthusiastically to get the attention of a waiter at the other side of the room.

"I'm Talia. Pleased to meet you."

"What would you like?" Perin asked excitedly.

"I'm not sure," said Talia as she hastily scanned the menu already at the table. "There's so much to choose from."

"Don't worry," Perin said kindly. "Let's order a little bit of everything. That way, you can try a selection."

When the waiter arrived, Perin immediately began rattling off a list of various dishes, much to Talia's surprise, considering what it would cost.

Once the waiter had dutifully walked away, Perin noticed Talia's expression.

"My father is highly regarded around here," she explained. "I don't mean to boast, but the chef is always happy to prepare a few extra dishes for me."

"What does your father do?" Talia asked.

"He's the head professor at Rosethorn Academy. It's not far from here."

"Are you serious?!" Talia exclaimed, her eyes widening in surprise.

"Is there a problem?" Perin asked, suspiciously raising an eyebrow.

For a moment, Talia sat in stunned silence.

"Are you alright?" Perin eventually asked.

"I've always wanted to go to Rosethorn Academy," Talia said passionately. "It's been my dream for so long! I've walked all night and nearly all day to get to Priggly from my village."

"That's amazing!" Perin exclaimed, a wide grin spreading across her face. "You must be very determined."

"Do you happen to know how I can apply?" Talia asked. "Is there some sort of screening process?"

"Don't you know?" Perin asked, surprised.

Feeling embarrassed, Talia shook her head. In response, Perin quickly waved her hand dismissively, as if to brush off the shame.

"Don't worry," she said firmly. "I'll speak to my father, and we'll make sure you get in.

Typically, there is an application process, but we can find a way around it. I can tell you're truly committed to this. Do you have money for tuition?"

Talia looked down at the table and shook her head, her hopes beginning to fade.

"It's ok," said Perin. "We'll work it out. I promise we'll get you into the academy. Its teachings are so wonderful; I want them to be accessible rather than elusive. We'll spend the night here, and then tomorrow, we'll go and talk to my father."

"Thank you," Talia said humbly, overwhelmed with gratitude, but not quite sure how to express it.

"Anytime," Perin replied with a friendly smile.

"Do you live nearby?" Talia asked, still in disbelief about the generous offer.

"Yeah," said Perin.

"I thought you might. Why are you staying at the tavern?"

"I usually stay here whenever my parents have guests over. Father is holding a board meeting. Staying at The Enchanted Acorn spares me from having to endure a dreadfully dull evening with a group of uptight diplomats."

Before Perin could elaborate, the waiter arrived with a vast assortment of food and drinks. Talia was looking forward to tucking in.

"Here's to new friendships," she said cheerfully, lifting her glass for a toast.

"Cheers to that!" said Perin, raising her own glass in agreement.

Chapter Five

After getting comfortable in their room, Talia and Perin talked late into the night. Perin shared anecdotes about her upbringing around magic; both her parents held positions at Rosethorn Academy – her father as the head professor, and her mother as an administrator. Perin told Talia enchanting tales of academy alumni who had gone on to do amazing and worthwhile things. Some had gone on to work as healers, whilst others had gone on to teach.

"I hadn't even thought about what I would do if I ever graduated from Rosethorn Academy," Talia said, feeling drowsy and content as she lay in bed gazing up at the ceiling. "Just being there and being surrounded by magic and like-minded fae would be enough for me."

"Dream big, Talia," Perin said. "There are so many wonderful things that can be done with the magic of a rose thorn. It takes a lot of study, and a lot of practice, but when you see the results, they are phenomenal. Anything that can help others has got to be worth striving for."

Having felt compelled to minimise her ambitions for so long, talking with Perin was a breath of fresh air for Talia.

"How much magic have you done so far?" she asked.

"Admittedly, not that much," said Perin. "There's a lot of theory work to do beforehand. The classes get more advanced over time; there's a lot to learn. When magic goes wrong, it can go *really* wrong."

"Oh?"

"You don't need to worry though. The teachers know what they're doing, and there's always somebody around to ask – even if you just go to one of the more advanced students."

Talia smiled, sensing that Perin had a desire to mentor her.

"Anyway, we should get some rest now," said Perin. "I'm looking forward to introducing you to the academy tomorrow."

With that, they settled down to go to sleep. Although Talia was tired, she didn't immediately drift off. Instead, she stayed awake for a little while, excited for the future.

***

Talia could feel somebody shaking her shoulder.

"Talia! Wake up!"

"Just a few more minutes, Mother," she replied, her voice thick with sleep as she turned away to snuggle beneath the blanket, still too groggy to realise that she was not in her childhood bedroom.

"Talia!" Perin exclaimed, amusement in her tone. "I'm not your mother!"

Now aware of her surroundings, Talia turned around and opened her eyes.

"Rise and shine!" Perin said cheerfully. "Let's go down for breakfast. After that, we'll go to the academy."

Talia leapt up and quickly got ready. In a matter of minutes, she found herself following Perin down the stairs into the heart of the tavern.

"I've already ordered some pancakes for you," Perin said as they took a seat at a nearby table. "Is that ok?"

Talia nodded with enthusiasm, her wings catching the faint glow coming from a string of lights hanging along the wall.

"Fantastic!" said Perin. "I'll be taking you on a tour of the academy today! You're going to love it."

As the waiter came by to serve breakfast, Talia was taken aback by the sheer volume of it. The thick pancakes were stacked high, drizzled with a generous amount of syrup.

"We'll head over to the academy as soon as we've finished eating," Perin said with her mouth full. "We'll go to my father's office right away, and I can talk to him about getting you enrolled. After that, I can show you around. I assume you'll want to board there?"

Having taken a large bite of her delicious breakfast, Talia nodded.

"Rosethorn Academy is huge," said Perin. "There's plenty of space for those who want to live there. Some students prefer to live off-campus, so we always have rooms available for new students."

"That's good," said Talia, her brow furrowing as a worrying thought occurred to her. "How much will it cost?"

"Don't worry," Perin said with certainty. "We'll sort something out with my father."

When the pair finished their meal, they paid the bartender, and then made their way outside into the bustling town.

As Perin took the lead, Talia trailed closely behind. She had little interest in the shop windows and vendors that they passed, her thoughts dominated by her desire to get to the academy.

"We'll be there in no time," said Perin, sensing Talia's eagerness.

As they continued their stroll through Priggly, Perin keenly pointed out her favourite landmarks.

"Over there is the bookstore, owned by Mrs Doyle. She's really kind and welcoming; she lets you read in there without any obligation to make a purchase. Next to it is Mr Smyth's store, which sells outdoor supplies. If you're in need of anything related to the great outdoors, he's your go-to guy – if he doesn't have it, no one else will. Oh, and that building over there... a few students from the academy live there. It's a nice place for fae who would rather not live on campus."

"Where's the academy?" Talia asked, becoming more impatient.

"It's at the very edge of town, right near the forest – a perfect location for gathering wildflowers. Within the walls of the academy, we have plenty of gardens too, sof course. Equally though, it's lovely to live so close to all kinds of flora and fauna."

"It's lovely to think that you've lived there all your life."

"Oh yes," said Perin. "I feel very lucky for it too. Rosethorn Academy has been around for hundreds of years. Most of my ancestors had the privilege of studying there."

"I wonder how it was first figured out that the magic of flowers can be harnessed – especially roses; they're so beautiful."

"I'd like to believe that the ancient fae were guided by magic itself," Perin said with a smile. "We're so lucky now that the answers have been passed from generation to generation. That said though, there's still probably a lot that nobody knows."

"That's amazing," said Talia.

Although she couldn't help but feel a flutter of unease about how much there was to learn, overall, she felt inspired.

Chapter Six

As they neared the threshold of Rosethorn Academy, Talia's eyes widened in amazement. The grandeur before her was beyond anything she could have ever imagined. It was gated with iron bars that loomed tall and formidable, as if guarding the secrets of the ancient knowledge held inside. Ivy, verdant and lush, was wrapped tightly around each bar, as if nature itself sought to endorse the magic within.

Beyond the gates, Talia could see a grand old building that seemed to stretch up to the sky. There were smaller buildings connected to it. With stunning gardens in bright bloom all around, the air was thick with the sweet scent of blossoming flowers and the earthy aroma of dew-kissed grass.

Her gaze fixed on the awe-inspiring sight, Talia felt a rush of excitement at the thought of being able to study at such an incredible place. She felt as though she had stepped into a different world, as though she had entered a peaceful haven, a place where time had slowed down to allow for nature to truly shine. She closed her eyes and breathed deeply, feeling a sense of calm and serenity that she had never experienced before. Being around nature had a way of making her feel at ease; she knew that she would never tire of learning about its unique powers.

"It's impressive, isn't it?" Perin said proudly. "Let's go inside. I would hate for you to miss the opportunity of speaking with my father."

With a determined push, Perin exerted her strength against the gate barring their path to the academy. Her wings twitched behind her, testament to the momentum of her efforts as she strained against the weight of the metal. As it slowly gave way, its hinges groaned and creaked.

"It's always pretty quiet at the weekend," she said. "There won't be many fae around at the moment."

As they strolled up the pathway leading towards the main building, Talia's eyes lit up in wonder. The grand structure that loomed before them was nothing short of extraordinary.

"The orchids are blooming beautifully, and so is the lavender," Perin said as she pointed out one of the many smaller gardens. "They are probably for some of the more advanced students to use in their practical magic classes."

Talia had often fantasised about practicing magic, but the notion of it ever becoming a reality had always seemed so far beyond her reach.

I can't believe I'm finally here!

Gazing up at the imposing building towering above them, Talia watched as Perin strode up the stone steps to ring the doorbell. Soon enough, the door was flung open by a fae with flowing blonde hair, who appeared to be no more than sixteen years old.

"Hello Perin!" the young fae greeted with an enormous smile. "Who's your friend?"

"Talia, meet Ruby," Perin said. "She's the younger sister of one of our teachers here at the academy. She'll be an official student in a year or two."

Ruby simply nodded, seemingly unperturbed by Perin's description of her.

"Ruby, this is Talia," said Perin. "I'm determined to persuade my father to enrol her."

"Delighted to have you here, Talia!" said Ruby, accompanied by a polite flutter of her sky-blue wings. "Please, come in."

As Talia stepped into the grand entrance hall of the building, she looked around in amazement. The towering ceilings and magnificent stained-glass windows featured vibrant designs of roses. The staircase ahead of her seemed to stretch up into the heavens, serving to make the interior appear even more enormous than the outside.

She was quickly pulled from her reverie when, without hesitation, Perin took hold of her hand and led her inside the first room on the right, which turned out to be an office. It was tastefully decorated with rose-themed wallpaper, with several framed portraits dotted about, each of them featuring fae who appeared to be important figures. The emerald-green carpet felt luxuriously soft beneath Talia's feet, reminiscent of lush long grass.

To the back of the office, tucked within a smaller room, was a stately mahogany desk. Behind it, sat a man who exuded an air of authority, his appearance suggesting that he was in his mid-fifties. With his iridescent wings folded gracefully behind his back, his attention was absorbed by the paperwork spread before him, which he gazed upon through wide-rimmed glasses perched on the tip of his nose.

"Father?" Perin enquired, her tone respectful and cautious.

In a silent gesture that told Perin to wait, he raised his finger. Talia didn't mind. The pause afforded her the opportunity to further examine the room. The spacious office had two grand windows: one offered a stunning view of the gardens, whilst through the other was the seemingly endless forest.

After a while, Perin's father lifted his head from his paperwork.

"Yes, Perin," he said in a friendly and approachable tone. "What can I do for you?"

"Father, I want you to meet Talia. She's a new friend of mine. Talia, this is Reginald Thistle, the head professor of Rosethorn Academy."

Talia followed Perin's example and stepped closer to the desk.

"Hello, Professor," she said in a subdued tone, feeling somewhat awkward and out of place.

"Pleased to meet you, Talia," he greeted, his tone brimming with warmth and putting her at ease.

"Talia's interested in becoming a student here," said Perin.

"Oh?" he uttered, a hint of uncertainty in his voice. "Have you submitted your application, Talia?"

Before Talia could answer, Perin spoke on her behalf.

"She hasn't yet, but she's made a huge effort to be here and has given up a lot for this opportunity. Also, she's my friend. Can't we let her stay, please?"

"Do you have a passion for magic?" Professor Thistle asked Talia, carefully observing her anxious expression. "Will you only use it for good? At Rosethorn Academy, that's precisely what we learn. The magic of plants can be used for all kinds of purposes, but in the wrong hands, awful things can happen. We're only interested in using magic to benefit everyone involved. Is that something you agree with?"

"Yes, Professor," said Talia. "I'm willing to do whatever it takes to learn about magic. I've been fascinated by it for years. I can't imagine wanting to use it for anything other than good."

Although she had prepared a lengthier speech, it seemed that Professor Thistle had heard everything he needed.

"Do you have the funds for your room and board?" he asked.

"I'm not sure," Talia answered sincerely. "How much would it cost?"

Professor Thistle leaned back in his chair, his gaze, though gentle, holding a hint of concern as he observed Talia.

"Hmm…" he mused. "I can see that you very much want to be here. Would you be willing to work around the premises in exchange for your room and board?"

"Yes, Professor," she replied, appreciative of the kind offer. "I promise to work hard."

"Alright," he said. "It appears we have an agreement. I can tell that you have a sincere passion for what we can offer you here at Rosethorn Academy. I am always eager to assist students who can contribute to our mission and values."

"Can Talia share my room with me?" Perin asked excitedly.

"Yes," he said. "Would that work for you, Talia?"

"It would," Talia replied. "Thank you."

"Very well," he said. "Perin, show Talia to her room."

"Thank you, Professor Thistle," Talia said humbly. "I'm determined to make the most of this opportunity. It means so much to me."

Chapter Seven

Talia followed Perin through the quiet corridors of the academy. The tall windows adorned with intricate floral patterns bathed them in a soft, ethereal light, casting shadows that danced along the walls as they walked. Finally, after ascending several flights of stairs, they reached Perin's room. Hanging on the door was a wreath of dried flowers, their colours still vivid despite the passage of time.

"Here we are," said Perin as she pushed the door open.

Filled with an abundance of plants and flowers, the scent of the room was incredible. The walls were decorated with a mural of vines and branches that reached up towards the ceiling. Behind the headboards of the two single beds, the mural depicted a wild meadow with butterflies.

"I've had this space all to myself for quite a while," said Perin. "I'm happy to share it with you."

"Thank you," said Talia.

"If there's anything else you need, we can make a trip into town another day."

"That's good. What do I need to do today? Should I enrol in a certain class? Who do I need to see?"

Perin flopped out onto her bed, which was scattered with books and clothes.

"Don't worry about that for now," she said. "Take a breather and get comfortable. Dinner will be served shortly. I can take you on a guided tour en route. You'll start classes tomorrow."

Talia, visibly relieved, gave a small nod. Perin then lazily shifted her position on the bed, stretching and yawning before wrapping herself around a large pillow.

"I need a quick nap," she said, unable to suppress a yawn.

Perin's need for a break provided Talia with a chance to settle in. She set her bag by her bed and went to the window. From there, she could make out the town in the distance. As she stared at the road on which she and Perin had travelled, it reminded her of how far she was from home, which caused her to think of her parents.

Finally, she was exactly where she had wanted to be for so long, and yet she couldn't shake the feeling that something was missing. No matter how hard she tried to tell herself to be positive, an intrusive sense of homesickness touched at the corners of her mind.

Taking the initiative, she turned her focus to the present. She knew that she would need to demonstrate her value if she was going to stay at the academy. With that in mind, she turned away from the window and tiptoed out of the bedroom, leaving Perin to snooze in peace.

Walking alone through the academy, as she descended several flights of stairs, Talia was greeted by the pleasant smell of baking. Deciding to follow it, she found herself on an unfamiliar floor, the stained-glass windows casting a kaleidoscope of beautiful rainbow patterns all around.

"Hello," called a female voice that Talia didn't recognise.

As she turned to look at the woman, Talia instantly felt at ease. With a warm smile accentuating the apples of her chubby cheeks, the older woman wore an apron covered in food stains – even her pearlescent-peach wings had a dusting of flour upon them. She held a bowl in her hands, no doubt a sign that she was a cook. A pleasant twinkle in her eye, she gave Talia a friendly nod.

"I'm Heather," she said. "I don't think we've met before. You must be new here."

"I am. I'm Talia. I don't suppose you need any help in the kitchen? I want to work in order to pay for my board here."

"Can you cook?"

"I'm not too bad at it. If there's something I don't know, I'll gladly learn."

"Very well," said Heather. "You can be my assistant in the kitchen – before and after mealtimes."

"I'll enjoy that," said Talia. "Whatever it is you're baking at the moment, it smells wonderful."

"Follow me," said Heather, her tone bright and welcoming. "Let's bake the bread for tonight's meal."

Eager to put her best foot forward, Talia trailed behind Heather as they made their way to the kitchen.

***

"We can go down there at night to get snacks," Perin said excitedly, pleased that Talia had secured a job in the kitchen. "You could also bring leftovers up to our room."

"Fantastic," Talia said as she proudly presented a bag of baked goods that Heather had bundled together for her. "Great minds think alike."

With a twinkle in her eyes, Perin jubilantly

bounced up from her bed, keen to examine the offering that Talia had brought up to their room.

"I'm pretty pleased with how the bread turned out," Talia said, happy that she had been an asset to Heather. "There was quite a bit left over, in fact, and..."

Eager to eat, Perin dismissed Talia's explanation with a wave of her hand.

"Heather's great," she said, taking a bite of a roll. "She's easygoing, and will be nice about it when you need time off for something. She's not a pushover; she's kind."

"It's lucky that I bumped into her in the hallway," said Talia. "But, hey, let's not eat all of the bread now. There's a delicious casserole for dinner. It would be a shame to fill up on bread and miss out on that."

***

Talia and Perin concluded their evening with a hearty meal, followed by a brief stroll through just some of the academy before heading back to their room for the night.

"You've got a big day ahead tomorrow," said Perin. "We should try to get some sleep."

With a nod, Talia settled into bed, tightly wrapping the duvet around her. As soon as she closed her eyes, she entered a long, deep sleep that would see her through to the morning.

Chapter Eight

"Rise and shine!" Perin said in a loud sing-song voice as she gave Talia's shoulder a gentle shake. "We need to get a move on! We're already late!"

Rubbing the sleep from her eyes, Talia shuffled out of bed. Perin hastily handed her a pile of neatly folded clothes. As Talia began to unfold them, she realised that it was a uniform – a pleated checked skirt, a black-and-white-striped tie, a dark woolly jumper, and a white long-sleeved button-up shirt. Just as Talia had finished laying out the outfit on her bed, Perin proudly thrust a gold-coloured broach into her hand. Noticing the enamel design on it, which featured the academy's emblem, Talia couldn't help but pause to quickly read the mantra beneath it:

In thorns we trust.

Curious to know more, but pressed for time, she scrambled to get dressed. She then slipped her feet into the polished shoes she had packed, and took a quick moment to brush her hair in front of the mirror.

As they dashed down the stairs, she caught sight of a throng of other students, many of whom seemed to be in their twenties. All of them had the same drowsy-yet-determined expressions etched on their faces. The sheer size of the crowd served to remind Talia that an education from Rosethorn Academy was sought by many.

"I'll gladly introduce you to more students during breakfast," Perin said with a grin.

"I ought to pop by the kitchen to see Heather first," Talia replied.

Perin hesitated, but after a brief pause, she nodded in agreement.

"Sure," she said. "I'll see you later, either in the dining room, or if not, Heather can tell you where to go for your first class."

With an excited twitch of her wings, Perin

then darted away, keen to catch up with everyone else.

Entering the kitchen, Talia was met with a chaotic scene. Heather was standing by a stove with all the burners blazing, simultaneously cooking a pancake with one hand, whilst tending to some scrambled eggs with the other. Other burners were occupied with bacon and black pudding.

"Good morning, Talia!" Heather said cheerfully. "I was hoping you would drop by!"

"Sorry I'm late," Talia replied. "I overslept."

"Well, no problem; it was your first night here, after all," Heather reassured. "However, we'll need to talk about you getting up a bit earlier to assist me in making breakfast from now on."

"I promise I will," said Talia. "I grew up on a farm, so I'm used to getting up early."

"Turn the bacon over and tell me about it."

As they cooked breakfast together, Talia shared her life story with Heather, flipping bacon, black pudding, and pancakes in between. As they piled the food onto plates and drizzled syrup over the pancakes, Heather reciprocated by telling Talia about how she had come to be at the academy.

"When I was just a girl, the magic of a rose thorn saved my mother's life," Heather explained. "She was gravely ill with a broken wing. She was running such a fever that my father and I were terrified she wouldn't survive. We were incredibly lucky that someone put us in touch with a healer several villages over. She travelled quickly to us, having picked a beautiful rose along the way. As soon as she arrived, she held one of the thorns between her forefinger and thumb, focusing all of her energy onto it. With her hand surrounded by a warm glow, she touched my mother's forehead, causing her fever to break and her wing to knit together. By using the magical power of a rose thorn, that fae saved my mother's life."

"That's incredible," said Talia, touched by what had happened.

"Yes," said Heather. "After that, I knew that I wanted to stand in support of such magic, and it just so happens that I'm not a bad cook!"

Wow!

"If you put those plates through the hatch, the students can help themselves. I've already put the coffee, tea, and juice out for them," Heather explained. "We can have our meal here if you like. Don't feel that you have to though. You might prefer to go and join the others."

"I'll enjoy eating breakfast with you," Talia told Heather, keen to continue their conversation.

"Here you go," said Heather, sliding a plate across to Talia. "There's plenty more if you fancy seconds."

"This is delicious," Talia said as she tucked in.

"Thank you," Heather said modestly, blushing slightly. "You're very welcome. I must say, it's great to have another pair of hands in the kitchen."

Taking Talia by surprise, a bell rang out from somewhere within the academy.

"That's the bell for first period," said Heather. "Your first class is on the second floor. Once you're there, take the third door on the right. Don't worry about the washing-up – you're running late enough as it is. Just make sure you come back here for lunch."

There was so much that Talia wanted to ask Heather. Not only was she fascinating to listen to, but she seemed so knowledgeable. Still though, Talia hated the thought of being late for her first class.

"Thanks, Heather," she called out, already on her way out of the kitchen.

As she rushed up the stairs to the second floor, she cleaned herself up. Despite her efforts, she missed a few spots of flour, and by the time she got to the door of the classroom, her jumper was still marked with a syrup stain.

Chapter Nine

Talia pushed open the door to the classroom. Wooden desks and chairs formed neat rows, all of which faced a chalkboard at the front of the room. The majority of students had already settled in their seats. Glancing around nervously, Talia was pleased to see a familiar face approaching.

"Hey, Talia," said Perin, speaking quickly and sounding slightly out of breath. "I was wondering where you had got to! Just so you know, this isn't my class. I took it a couple of years back. It's mandatory for everyone when they start. Anyway, once the class is over, let's meet in the hallway. You're with me for second period."

Before Talia could even think to respond, Perin hastily left the room, no doubt in a rush to get to her own class.

Where should I sit?

Hovering by the door and overthinking the scenario, Talia's attention was soon drawn to the teacher who entered the room. A middle-aged woman with flame-red hair, she had snazzy, colourful glasses on the very tip of her slender nose. Her wings were a beautiful shade of magenta. She was cradling a generous pile of books under one arm, while gripping a cup of coffee with her other hand.

"Good morning, everyone," she greeted. "I hope you all had a good weeken... Oh! You must be Talia?"

Talia nodded, shy, but pleased to be acknowledged.

"I'm Mrs Gould. I'll be your teacher for Introduction to Magic Studies. It's a mandatory course for all incoming students. There's a free seat towards the back, next to Beagan."

Mrs Gould motioned towards the empty chair next to a slender, pale young fae sitting near the back of the classroom. Talia smiled and proceeded to walk over to him. When he returned the expression in kind, his delicate features flattering his overall demeanour, she sensed that she could relax.

"Ok, class," said Mrs Gould, demanding everyone's attention with the authority in her tone. "Now, I know that most of you already know this, but let's review the fundamentals. Firstly, what qualifies as magic?"

"Ugh!" a young woman seated in front of Talia groaned in frustration. "Everyone already knows this!"

"I would appreciate a recap," said Beagan, speaking up in a loud voice that betrayed his slight physique.

He winked kindly at Talia. She nodded at him gratefully before redirecting her attention back to their teacher.

As Mrs Gould discussed the various types of plants and their magical properties, Talia was captivated. The subject was far broader than she had imagined. She meticulously transcribed every detail in her notebook, sketching diagrams of several flowers.

"Now then," said Mrs Gould, her tone turning dark and giving everyone in the room cause to take their eyes off their books. "Not everyone respects the moral and ethical responsibilities that should be embraced when practising magic. Some fae use it for bad deeds rather than good. The Sprightlys are a prime example of this. They use magic for the sole purpose of intimidation. For of course, in the wrong hands, magic can be used for destruction – pillaging towns, burning villages. At Rosethorn Academy, our duty is to train intelligent and resourceful practitioners who only use magic for good, and who will speak out against the harm caused by groups like the Sprightlys."

Almost involuntarily, Talia raised her hand.

"Yes, Talia?" Mrs Gould enquired.

"Can we do any more than speaking against them?" Talia asked. "Couldn't we use magic to overpower their unreasonable use of it?"

"Absolutely not," Mrs Gould replied. "That would make us no better than the Sprightlys. We have to keep the moral high ground. We have to be better than them by setting a positive example and…"

"But what good does that do?" Talia interjected. "Surely we should try and stop them."

Immediately worried that she may have spoken out of turn, Talia gasped.

"I'm ever so sorry," she said, anxious to be more humble in her approach. "It's just that it's so disheartening to know that something as powerful as magic isn't always used for good. With bad fae having used it as a tool for terrorism, it's no wonder that some innocent fae are suspicious of something that could be helpful to them in the right hands."

Everyone's gaze was fixed on Mrs Gould in anticipation of an answer. It took her a moment to gather her thoughts before giving a response.

"It's ok, Talia," she said. "The questions you're asking are not unreasonable. It shows that you are passionate, and that you care. Ultimately, choosing to set a good example may not seem impactful, but it's better than resorting to violence. Using magic for anything other than good would make us no better than the Sprightlys."

"But what the Sprightlys are doing is unacceptable," said Talia, becoming more invested in the debate and convinced of the validity of her argument. "Surely it puts us in the wrong by choosing to do nothing. If using magic against the Sprightlys is the only way to stop them, then maybe it could be justified."

"I'm impressed with your engagement today, Talia," said Mrs Gould, her tone sincere. "But remember: two wrongs can never make a right. That's it for today's lesson though. We've just about run out of time."

As if right on cue, the bell rang, indicating the conclusion of first period. Talia picked up her things and made her way out of the classroom.

"You presented a compelling argument," Beagan said with conviction as he caught up with her, taking brisk strides. "The Sprightlys have been misusing magic for far too long. It's high time they were held accountable."

"It seems crazy to me that anyone would want to sit back and let them get away with it," said Talia.

"Maybe one day, you could take them on yourself," Beagan suggested. "In the not-too-distant future, the magic will be in your hands."

Before Talia could entertain the exhilarating prospect of wielding magic herself, she was brought back to reality upon hearing her name.

"Hey, Talia!" Perin called out from the other end of the corridor as she approached. "How did your first class go?"

"It was certainly an experience," Talia remarked. "Perin, do you know Beagan?"

"Oh, I've seen you around before," Perin said cheerfully to Beagan. "It's great to properly meet you though!"

"It's a pleasure to meet you as well, Perin," said Beagan.

"We'd better get a move on, Talia," said Perin.

"We don't want to be late for second period. You're with me for that, and for period three as well. After you've finished helping Heather in the kitchen for lunch, we could go outside for some fresh air. After that, we have two more periods before dinner. I'll make sure you get to all of them on time – you're with me for those too. And don't worry; you'll get used to the schedule in no time."

"Thanks, Perin," Talia said appreciatively.

"You're welcome," said Perin.

After uttering a rushed goodbye to Beagan, Talia hurried along after Perin to their next class.

Chapter Ten

By the time lessons had ended for the day, Talia's mind was whirling. There had been so much to take in. She had made lots of notes, and knew that she would have to read back over them in order to understand everything.

Magic was far more complex than she had been expecting. The use of plants had been the subject of research and record-keeping for hundreds of years. Not only did different plants hold different magical powers, but they all had to be cared for in a particular way. For any fae wishing to practise magic, there were also moral and ethical points to consider. Overall, Talia felt as though she had been transported to an entirely different world to the one she had become used to back home at the farm.

"How are you finding it all?" Heather asked as she organised the kitchen in preparation for the evening meal.

With a heavy sigh, Talia plonked herself down onto a wooden chair. Her movements fuelled by sheer exasperation, the seat creaked beneath her.

"I'm glad to be here," she said. "But I would be lying if I said I wasn't overwhelmed. There's so much to take in. It feels as though everyone else is so far ahead, and that it will take me ages to catch up."

"That's first days for you," Heather said kindly. "Don't panic. I'm sure you'll pick everything up quickly – just like you have with me, here in the kitchen. Your passion and desire to learn will carry you through. Besides, nobody knows everything about magic. We're all still learning, really. If there's anything you're not sure about, don't hesitate to ask."

"Thanks, Heather," Talia said gratefully. "I'm sure you're right. It has been quite a hectic day."

"Let's get started on dinner," said Heather, clapping her hands together with enthusiasm as if trying to break through Talia's worried train of thought. "We're having grilled cheese sandwiches and tomato soup tonight. The soup's already prepared, so you can start serving it into those bowls over there. I'll work on the sandwiches."

Comforted by Heather's reassuring demeanour, Talia got up, grabbed a ladle, and diligently got to work.

"If it helps, you could talk me through what you're learning," Heather suggested as she grated a block of cheese into fine wisps. "Sometimes it can be helpful to break these things down."

"Of all the things I've picked up today, the thing that's really stayed with me is what Mrs Gould told us about the Sprightlys," said Talia, lines of concern etched on her forehead.

"Ah, yes," Heather said regretfully. "I'm not surprised. It's upsetting to think of the awful things some fae do with magic."

"Why hasn't anyone tried to stop them?" Talia asked, her tone laced with exasperation.

"Many have tried, but none have succeeded," Heather said sadly. "The trouble with the Sprightlys is that there are many of them, and over the years, they have mastered their craft. When it comes to using magic to wage war on innocent fae, the Sprightlys are devastatingly good at what they do. If they see a village that they wish to raid, with the power of magic behind them, they'll simply swoop in and take whatever they want."

"It's disgusting," said Talia, feeling a shudder of rage creeping along her spine. "It gives magic a bad name. No wonder the fae back home in Calyun are so against it."

"Indeed," said Heather. "Nobody should look to the Sprightlys as an example of how to use magic. Sadly though, it's all that some fae have ever known."

"Calyun has never been raided in my lifetime," Talia said. "Perhaps that's why I have always been more open to magic than some of the older generations there."

"That's certainly possible," said Heather.

As Talia continued to methodically ladle the steaming tomato soup into bowls, her mind was a whirlwind, each thought vying for attention amidst the steady rhythm of her task that blended with the sizzle of sandwiches being fried. Deep in contemplation, she simply couldn't ignore the complexities of magic and the troubling revelations about the Sprightlys she had encountered earlier in the day, causing her to grapple with questions of morality and responsibility.

"Something needs to be done," she said.

"I'm afraid there's little we can do," said Heather, resignation in her voice. "Let's not dwell on it. Have you finished serving the soup?"

"Yes."

"Fantastic. Come and help me to plate-up these sandwiches."

"Ok," Talia replied as she walked over to the other side of the kitchen.

"When it comes to the Sprightlys' terrorism, and whether anything could be done to stop them, I don't know what the answer is," Heather said earnestly. "I must say though, Talia, that I admire your passion and willingness to question things."

Chapter Eleven

As time passed and weeks turned into months, Talia devoted herself to her studies. Even when going for a walk into town with Perin, she often chose to read over her notes when sitting down for a coffee.

Talia was used to working hard, and because she enjoyed studying, it didn't feel like a burden in the slightest. She adored being challenged by her teachers, welcoming the opportunity to improve her knowledge. Everyone – including the other students – was impressed with her positive approach to learning, and by the insightful questions she often asked. Finally able to dedicate herself towards something that felt worthwhile, for the first time in her life, Talia was happy.

As she entered the classroom with her fellow students, there was a buzz of excitement in the air. The tall windows let in streams of warm sunlight, casting a glow over the rows of wooden desks. From the elegant display that lined the room, came the inviting fragrance of flowers. There were fresh tulips, lilies, and daisies, the petals on all of them radiating their potential for magic.

Talia and Beagan sat down next to each other, eagerly anticipating the lesson.

"I've been looking forward to this for so long," said Talia.

"Me too," said Beagan with an excited twitch of his wings.

Right on time for the lesson, in walked Mrs Gould, her long flame-red hair pulled back in a voluminous braid.

"Good morning, everyone," she greeted. "Today, we'll be exploring the magical properties of tulips. Before we get started, I just want to remind you all that you're here because you passed the theory test. As we progress through this class, it is imperative that you don't forget everything that you had to learn. I promise that it will come in handy as we get started on your practical training."

Talia exchanged a grin with Beagan and then quickly turned her attention back to Mrs Gould. She was determined not to miss out on even the smallest detail.

"Now," said Mrs Gould. "The vital thing about all magic, regardless of which plant you are working with, is that first and foremost, the power has to come from *you*. You have to be willing to channel all of your focus into what you're doing."

With determination in her stride, Mrs Gould walked over to a display table at the side of the room. With a delicate touch, she lifted a cobalt-blue ceramic vase of tulips, cradling it in her hands like a precious treasure. As she gently placed the vase on her desk before the eager eyes of her students, the tulips, in their colours of crimson, gold, and creamy-white, seemed to shimmer in the sunlight.

"Can anyone guess why we're starting out with tulips?" she asked. "Yes, Carrie?"

"Is it because they are less potent than rose thorns?" offered the young woman in the front row of seats.

"Yes. Well done, Carrie," said Mrs Gould. "That's exactly it. Whilst we must never underestimate the magical properties and potential of any plant, it is certainly the case that tulips are an excellent choice for beginners to start out with. Not only are they relatively easy to work with, but their propensity for chaos is minimal compared to, say, a rose thorn in the wrong hands."

Upon hearing this, Talia couldn't help but think about how much she wanted to take on the Sprightlys one day. Reminding herself that she was only just taking her first practical magic lesson though, she resolved to pay close attention.

"Ok, everyone," said Mrs Gould. "The first thing you need to do when approaching a plant for magic, is to look deep within yourself so that you can tune-in to the nature and energy of everything around you. With this in mind, don't be alarmed if I am quiet for a while as part of the demonstration I'm about to do. As you will soon realise for yourselves, the sensation of preparing for magic can feel extremely immersive."

She didn't need to ask for silence. The whole

class was already hanging on her every word. They watched in awe as she began her demonstration. Picking a single crimson petal from one of the tulips, she held it reverently, its soft, velvet texture resting between her forefinger and thumb. Then, she took a deep breath and closed her eyes, seeming to enter some kind of trance. As though responding to her energy, the petal began to quiver.

Suddenly, with a burst of light, the petal started to change. At first, it was a subtle shift, the vibrant crimson colour beginning to glow with flashes of intense magenta. Small electric-blue particles then began to dance around it, swirling and twisting as if they were alive.

The students gasped in amazement as they watched the petal transform before their eyes. Talia couldn't believe what she was seeing. It was as if the petal was alive and had an energy all of its own. She leaned forward in her seat, her features alight with wonder as she watched the spectacle unfold.

The particles continued to dance and swirl, forming mesmerising patterns and shapes.

The petals of the other tulips in the vase began to vibrate, as if they too were caught up in the magic of the moment.

Finally, with a soft sigh, Mrs Gould opened her eyes. The particles began to dissipate, and the petal returned to its original colour, but there was something different about it now. It seemed to shine with a warmth and vitality that it had not possessed before.

In the hushed silence of the classroom, some of the students looked as though they were on the verge of applause, their hands poised in mid-air. Others remained still, as if uncertain as to whether the sound of clapping would be obstructive. In the end, the silence lingered, each student lost in their own thoughts, processing the extraordinary event that had unfolded before them.

"Did you see that?!" Talia whispered to Beagan, unable to contain her excitement.

"Oh yes," he murmured. "That was incredible!"

Mrs Gould took a moment to centre herself. With a few gentle, deliberate breaths, she anchored her awareness to the present moment. Then, with a composed demeanour, she straightened her posture and cast a reassuring glance across the room. The aura of serenity that enveloped her seemed to radiate a calming influence, quietening the flutter of excitement and curiosity that buzzed among the students. Finally poised and collected, she prepared herself to address the class.

"Now that this petal is energised," she said, "it's important that I use it responsibly. With it having been used solely for the purpose of demonstration, the best thing to do is to let it out of the window and back into nature. It's sure to nourish whichever garden it lands on."

With that, she moved to the nearest window, a light breeze gently causing her magenta wings to flitter as she opened it. Extending her hand out with the petal resting on her palm, she waited patiently for the mild wind to carry it away.

"As you all know," she said, closing the window and returning to the front of the class, "the magic of tulips can be used to heal small wounds. It can also be used to enhance absorption of nutrients in young fae. Seeing as nobody in this classroom is in need of either of those things, the ethical thing is to send the petal back to the very garden from whence it came."

Talia looked down at her hands. There was a tiny cut on the back of her thumb where she had caught it on a drawer in the kitchen. She had been in a rush on that particular day, and had made a clumsy move.

"I've got a small wound," she announced, the words tumbling out of her mouth before she could stop them.

I desperately want to experience that magic for myself.

"Oh?" Mrs Gould uttered. "Well, Talia, my hand is still warm from the energy of having held that petal. May I touch my hand upon your wound? It would certainly heal it."

"Yes, please," said Talia, intrigued as to what it would feel like.

"Ok," said Mrs Gould.

With a generous smile, she walked up to Talia's desk. Everyone else in the room immediately gathered around to watch.

Closing her eyes, Mrs Gould extended her hand towards the small cut on Talia's thumb. Upon the first touch, a soft glow emanated from the point of contact.

Talia could feel a tingling, comforting sensation as the magic radiating from Mrs Gould flowed into her. Despite the fact that they were dealing with only a small wound, the overall sensation felt incredibly deep and profound.

As soon as Mrs Gould removed her hand from Talia's, the small cut began to close, eventually fading away as if it had never been there. Talia was astounded, as was everyone else.

"As you can see," said Mrs Gould as she took a step back to address the whole class, "tulips have subtle, yet effective healing properties."

Talia felt as though she had just witnessed something truly extraordinary. As the lesson continued, she felt inspired, longing to learn more about the magic of plants and the ways in which it could be used to help others.

If that's the kind of magic that can be accessed with a tulip, I can barely imagine how wondrous it must be to work with rose thorns!

Chapter Twelve

"Good morning, Heather," Talia said as she made her way into the kitchen.

She went to a hook on the wall and took down her apron. Heather had proudly sewn her name onto it not long after they had started working together.

"Morning, Talia," Heather greeted cheerfully. "How did you sleep?"

"Not very well," she admitted. "I was up most of the night, studying for the plant biology exam. It's tomorrow."

Heather tutted disapprovingly.

"Everyone needs a good nights' sleep," she said kindly. "It's good to relax. It seems to me that you hardly ever do."

"I like keeping busy though," Talia said innocently. "Besides, there's so much to learn."

"True," said Heather. "But don't forget to take a relaxing bath and get lost in a good book every so often. It will help to clear your head. I sense that you have a very busy mind at times."

"You can read me like a book," Talia said with a chuckle. "I really appreciate you looking out for me. Sometimes, I work myself up with so many thoughts and ideas, I'm surprised that I ever manage to get any sleep at all."

"I'll bet," said Heather. "I'm always here if you want to talk. Oh, and could you do me a favour and help with this salad? Professor Thistle has been on my case about not serving enough vegetables. If it's vegetables he wants, it's vegetables he'll get."

Talia smiled as Heather enthusiastically began to chop the cabbages.

"I'm sure he's happy with the food overall," she said, keen to offer reassurance as she set to work on the carrots.

"Oh yes," said Heather. "I wouldn't doubt it for a moment. If you ask me, it seems as though something has been bothering him recently."

"Oh?"

"I didn't want to pry," Heather added. "He and I have a good rapport. In fact, he has always been a wonderful friend to me. It's just that whatever it is, it seems to be upsetting him to the point of distraction."

"I see," said Talia, deep in thought.

I wonder what's bothering Professor Thistle. I'll always be grateful to him for having granted me a place here. I'd hate to think that he was struggling with something. Perhaps it's not my place to ask him lots of questions, but at the very least, I think I'll go to his office later and take him a coffee. Small things like that can do wonders during difficult times.

***

Once everything had been cleared away in the kitchen, Talia thanked Heather for her company. Having decided to follow through with her kind plan, holding a modest cup of coffee in one hand, she went down the flights of stairs towards Professor Thistle's office. When she got to the closed door, she used her free hand to straighten her uniform before knocking.

"Yes?" came the professor's voice from inside the office. "Come in."

Talia opened the door and slipped in.

"I've brought you some coffee, Professor," she said humbly as she moved forward to place it on his desk.

"Thank you, Talia," he said, appreciative, but his tone a little flat. "That's very kind of you. Please, take a seat."

As Talia settled into a chair opposite the Professor, who was sat behind his desk, she observed that he appeared disturbed, as though he had recently experienced something upsetting.

"Excuse me, Professor," she said softly, "but may I ask what's troubling you?"

Letting out a deep sigh, he sat forward in his chair and motioned towards a handwritten letter resting on his desk.

"This message is from a former student," he said gravely. "She lives in a town nearby; upon graduating, she returned there to educate others about magic."

"Oh?" Talia said cautiously, sensing that there was more to the story.

"Her entire town was destroyed by the Sprightlys," he said, his voice strained with emotion. "Despite her effort to defend it, she and the residential fae were outnumbered. Several lives were lost."

The professor placed his head in his hands, unable to maintain his composure. Talia's breath caught in her throat as she observed the usually-stoic fae. The air in the room felt heavier, suffocating her in its weighty silence. She sat frozen in her chair, unable to speak, her mind racing with the gravity of the news.

"The town is one of several neighbouring locations that the Sprightlys have attacked in recent years," said Professor Thistle, finally breaking the strained silence. "Their strategy involves targeting places not too distant from Rosethorn Academy. They seem to take pleasure in flaunting their triumphs at us."

With the professor's words sinking in, Talia's mind churned with conflicting thoughts. She knew that the teachings of Rosethorn Academy advocated for peace and restraint, even in the face of provocation. Yet, as she contemplated the dire reality of the devastation caused by the enemy, a fire ignited within her. It was high time, she thought, that the academy ceased its passive stance and took a stand against the Sprightlys' tyranny.

"Why can't we fight back?" she asked, her tone brimming with intensity.

"That's not our way of handling things," said Professor Thistle.

"I know," Talia pressed, sensing that the professor wasn't entirely convinced of his own words. "But what if the Sprightlys were to attack the academy? You would want to protect it, wouldn't you?"

"They won't attack us," he said, sounding more confident this time. "Although they made threats to do so many years ago, there is an indescribable quality about this place that shields us. It's why good fae with an affinity for magic are drawn here."

"Do you think your friend was in the wrong when she tried to defend her town?" Talia quizzed.

"Absolutely not," Professor Thistle said firmly. "She acted in self-defence. However, deploying fae from this academy to use vast surges of magic against the Sprightlys could not be considered self-defence. It would go against the very principles we strive to uphold."

"What if every town had a number of resident fae who were willing and able to protect it?"

"Where exactly are you going with this?" the professor asked, his eyebrow arched in suspicion.

"Why don't you assign some third-year students to live in the neighbouring towns?"

Talia suggested. "It could be an exchange programme, or a field trip of sorts. Then, in the event of an attack by the Sprightlys, nowhere would be without defence."

Looking at Talia intently, Professor Thistle pondered her proposition. Much to her disappointment though, after a moment, he shook his head in disagreement.

"That's not feasible," he said. "Our primary responsibility is to educate students about magic. Our focus is on promoting peace and harmony. It's not our role to engage in war with the Sprightlys."

"But fae are dying," Talia protested.

"Perhaps it's simply not our place to get involved," Professor Thistle said bluntly.

"You've got the authority to put an end to this," Talia said, her tone respectful, but with a hint of frustration. "We could prevent the Sprightlys from going on their raids. You have the power, and yet you're choosing to do nothing."

"Yes, but..."

"If it was my village or my family at risk, would you still choose to do nothing?" she asked, her voice rising with fury despite her respect for the professor. "Even the fact that every village and town is full of innocent fae with children: is that not enough to make you want to take action?!"

Talia could tell from Professor Thistle's expression that he had no answer for her. Just as she had stood up and was about to storm out of the office in anger, however, he finally spoke.

"I appreciate your concern, Talia, really I do. Please don't think that I'm not upset about what is happening. However, the Sprightlys and their abhorrent behaviour extends far beyond the influence of any individual or institution – ours included."

There was more that Talia wanted to say, but fearful that she would cross a line in speaking to the professor in sheer anger, all she could do was head out to the gardens in desperate need to clear her head.

Chapter Thirteen

With her mind still spinning from the intense conversation she'd just had with Professor Thistle, Talia was glad to be alone. She needed a moment to gather her thoughts.

Out in the academy gardens, she was amazed by the riot of colours that surrounded her, courtesy of the blooming flowers. Tall trees loomed above her, their branches reaching up towards the bright blue sky. Their leaves rustled gently in the breeze, casting dappled shadows across the ground. As she wandered down a winding path lined with hedges, a small pond came into view, its surface shimmering in the sunlight. Amongst the lilies floating lazily on the water, a family of ducks paddled about, seeming content in their environment.

Despite her idyllic surroundings, Talia was anything but content. She simply couldn't stop thinking about the dire behaviour of the Sprightlys. It disgusted and upset her to think that any fae could turn to such darkness.

Just after passing the pond, she was surprised to see Mrs Gould up ahead, positioned on her knees as she tended to a bed of flowers. As Talia walked closer to her, the friendly teacher looked up and smiled kindly.

"Hello, Talia," she said. "Are you ok? You look upset."

Talia wasn't quite sure what to say. She felt that it would be awkward to relay to Mrs Gould the difficult conversation that she'd just had with Professor Thistle.

"I'm ok," she lied. "I just fancied some fresh air and a walk."

"How about helping me turn this soil," Mrs Gould suggested. "I'm always happy to have a helping hand out here."

Grateful for the chance of a distraction, Talia quickly set to work, the soft grass pressing into her knees as she knelt beside the flowerbed. After a few moments though, she could no longer pretend that she wasn't brimming with questions.

"Mrs Gould," she said. "I'm ever so sorry, but I have to ask: I understand that we should never use magic for harm, but don't you think we should be willing to stop the likes of the Sprightlys – if only to protect the innocent?"

Causing wisps of her red hair to fall into her face, Mrs Gould shook her head gently, sympathetic to Talia's question rather than annoyed by it. Talia had, after all, asked similar questions in class.

"Talia," she said patiently, "violence only leads to more violence. If we were to use magic to stop the Sprightlys, it would make us no better than them. The true test of a good fae is in their ability to find peaceful solutions."

"But what about when there is no other way to help innocent bystanders as their homes are being raided?" Talia pressed.

Downing tools and turning away from their

flowerbed to meet Talia's gaze, Mrs Gould gently placed a hand on her shoulder.

"There is always a peaceful solution, Talia. It may not be easy, and it may not be immediate, but it is always possible. We must have faith in our abilities, and in the power of magic to heal even the most broken of hearts."

Talia sighed. She was frustrated, but she still had great admiration and respect for Mrs Gould.

"I understand," she said, unable to conceal her feelings of defeat. "I will try my best to always find a peaceful solution."

Mrs Gould smiled, her eyes shining with pride.

"That is all we can ask," she said. "Remember: the greatest strength any fae can have is in their determination to choose peace."

Mrs Gould is so sweet and patient. I don't want to force her into having a debate with me. I should take the opportunity to learn from her while I'm out here.

"These roses are looking lovely," Talia said. "I would imagine that there are many more out here."

"Oh yes," replied Mrs Gould. "In fact, I planted some more just yesterday. It's always good to have some around for the more experienced students' practical sessions."

"I'm looking forward to reaching that point myself."

"All in good time, Talia. First, you must master the fundamentals of magic. Only then can any fae begin to understand the true power of a rose thorn. Rose thorns are the most powerful of all the plants we can use for magic. They can give fae the power to fly higher, and for much longer than usual."

Talia's eyes widened as she listened to Mrs Gould's explanation. She knew that the taboo surrounding roses back in Calyun was such that she had much to learn.

"Not only that," Mrs Gould continued, "but rose thorn magic can also be used to shoot powerful and dangerous flames from one's hands. Of course, that's not something that we advise anyone to do. It's the very move used by the Sprightlys to start fires during their raids of towns and villages. They have even been known to shoot flames at innocent bystanders."

"The magic can be deadly," said Talia, more to herself than to Mrs Gould.

"Exactly," Mrs Gould confirmed. "That's why it's so important that a good fae never uses such power for harm. The magic is a gift, but it is also a responsibility. Use it wisely, and always for good."

Talia nodded in understanding, grateful for Mrs Gould's words of wisdom. The inspiring teacher had given her pause for thought. The calming surroundings of the academy gardens were certainly serving to help Talia's state of mind too. Focusing on their soothing embrace, she took a deep breath, telling herself to just be in the moment as she looked up towards the tall trees above.

As her gaze pierced the expanse of the sky, a flurry of movement caught her attention. At first, the shapes were mere blurs against the azure canvas, elusive and distant. Yet, as she strained her eyes and honed her focus, clarity dawned upon her, causing her heart to plummet with a sudden realisation: a sizable flock of fae were soaring swiftly overhead. She had never seen anything like it.

They moved menacingly, their wings slicing through the air with practiced ease. Their presence commanded attention, a domineering spectacle against the backdrop of the heavens. Talia's breath caught in her throat as she watched, her mind reeling with wonder and disbelief at the sheer scale of the sight unfolding before her.

"Is that..."

"The Sprightlys?" Mrs Gould interjected. "I'm afraid so."

A shiver of fear raced down Talia's spine. Having heard so much about the Sprightlys, to witness their presence firsthand was harrowing.

"They're heading in the direction of Calyun!" she cried out hysterically as she urgently jumped to a standing position. "That's my village!"

As the army of enemy fae continued to fly towards their destination, their wings beating ominously in the air, Talia knew that she had to do something, but felt helpless and unsure.

She glanced at Mrs Gould, hoping for reassurance, but the teacher's face was set in a grim expression, fear in her eyes. The reality of the situation had already set in for her.

Highly aware of what could happen if the Sprightlys in the sky weren't stopped, Talia felt sick with worry. She tried to calm herself down, to think optimistically, but it was no use. Her thoughts kept circling back to the destruction the Sprightlys could bestow upon her home, upon her family and friends.

As she stood there frozen in terror, she felt a hand on her shoulder. She turned around to see Mrs Gould standing beside her.

"I'm so sorry, Talia," she said gravely, her voice barely a whisper.

"Mrs Gould, please," Talia begged frantically. "We have to stop them. They're going to destroy everything."

Mrs Gould hesitated.

"Talia, as I've said before, we can't resort to violence. It goes against everything we stand for at Rosethorn Academy."

"But what choice do we have?" Talia said desperately. "We have to defend Calyun! It's my home! My family are there! They're defenceless!"

"I understand your concern," Mrs Gould said softly, "but rose thorn magic is not meant for battle. We can't use it for such purpose."

"Please, you have to help me," Talia pleaded. "I know we can't use magic for harm, but what about using it to protect? We can't just stand by and do nothing while they destroy everything."

"Talia, I understand how you feel, but you know that using rose thorn magic for battle goes against everything we stand for. It's dangerous, it's reckless, and it could have terrible consequences."

"I know, I know," Talia said, her eyes filling with tears. "But we have to protect Calyun from the Sprightlys. We have to do something – *anything* – to protect the innocent."

Mrs Gould exhaled a deep sigh, her expression making it clear that she acknowledged the validity of Talia's plea. The notion of employing magic for violence clashed with the very essence of her teachings, but it couldn't be denied that innocent fae would suffer, or possibly perish, if nothing was done.

"Ok," she conceded. "I'll help you, but we have to be careful; we must stick to a plan. We can't let ourselves be consumed by anger or fear, or we risk becoming just as bad as the Sprightlys. We must only use the minimum amount of force necessary to protect Calyun."

"Thank you," said Talia, her face lighting up with gratitude and relief. "Thank you so much."

With no time to lose, Mrs Gould crouched down and pressed her slender fingers into the soft earth closest to the roses nearby. Still attached to their stems, the thorns glistened in the sunlight. Without hesitation, she picked one, and then passed it to Talia.

"This is going to be intense," she warned. "Given the circumstances though, you're as ready for this as you'll ever be."

Gripping the precious thorn tightly between her trembling thumb and forefinger, Talia watched as Mrs Gould plucked another one from the same stem. Taking hold of her own thorn in the same position, the older woman focused her energy on it, and then closed her eyes in unwavering concentration.

Suddenly, the thorn in Mrs Gould's possession began to glow a bright shade of pink, pulsing with energy. When its glow swiftly changed to a vibrant shade of red, she held it to her chest. Her whole body began to shake with the power surging through her, causing her wings to twitch involuntarily. When she finally opened her eyes, they had a shine to them that seemed otherworldly.

Before Talia could muster a response, she felt Mrs Gould pressing the activated thorn against her forehead. Immediately, a jolt of energy rushed through Talia's body. As it coursed through her veins like lightning, she too started to vibrate with power. Feeling her wings tingling with the intensity of the magic, she stretched them wide, their dark-coloured tips taking on a phenomenal iridescence. Every fragment of her being crackled with a surge so overwhelming that it was almost painful.

Her pulse thumped with a combination of fear and determination. Not only had she experienced the enormity of rose thorn magic for the first time in her life, but she was about to fight for Calyun. She knew that the battle ahead would be dangerous and difficult, but she was willing to do whatever it would take to protect her loved ones and her home.

"Let's go," said Mrs Gould, taking Talia by the hand and leading her into the sky.

Chapter Fourteen

Talia could feel the wind rushing past her as she soared through the sky. Despite the dire circumstances, she marvelled at the feeling of being able to remain airborne with more ease than she had ever known before.

It took me days to walk this distance. I couldn't have flown it then, but now, the power of that rose thorn is making all the difference.

Comforted to know that she had such a skilled and powerful ally by her side, she glanced over at Mrs Gould. She had always been in awe of the inspiring teacher, but seeing her in action was truly something else; the way she glided effortlessly through the air, fully in control of her movements, was a sight to behold. It filled Talia with pride to know that Mrs Gould was willing to help her protect Calyun.

Her heart racing, Talia quickly turned her focus to what they were about to face. Still in shock that the Sprightlys had dared to even consider her humble home as their next target, her thoughts turned to her family and friends, and the possibility that they could be in grave danger.

I must protect them at all costs.

In an effort to avoid detection, Mrs Gould motioned for Talia to follow her on a slightly different route to the Sprightlys'. The pair flew a little higher in the sky. Keen to ensure that their presence in Calyun would take the enemy by surprise, they also knew that they needed to get there first.

"Turn left there," Talia called out to Mrs Gould as they neared their destination. "Follow the road when you see it, and then land in the centre of the village by that church building."

As Talia and Mrs Gould touched down on the cobblestones, their forms shimmering with the residual energy of the rose thorn magic, the piercing cry of a frightened woman shattered the air. The sound, raw, primal, and filled with terror and desperation, echoed through the quiet streets, tainting the atmosphere with an ominous sense of dread. Talia's heart lurched in her chest, her senses heightened by the sudden eruption of chaos. She exchanged an uncomfortable glance with Mrs Gould, ashamed that the fae of her village were afraid of them in their magic-enhanced state.

With no time to lose, Talia disregarded the frightened woman and bolted towards the village bell. Wrapping her fingers tightly around the cord, she pulled with all her might. The bell's urgent peal sliced through the air, summoning the attention of every fae in the vicinity.

Doors creaked open one by one, revealing anxious faces peering out into the uncertain disarray. Concerned murmurs rippled through the gathering crowd, their eyes wide with apprehension as they looked around for signs of danger. Talia could see the glint of makeshift weapons clutched tightly in trembling hands.

With a shared understanding that they would need to keep their own safety in mind, Talia and Mrs Gould beat their wings in order to gain a considerable height advantage before addressing everyone.

"Enemies are approaching!" Talia announced. "We're here to help. Don't hurt us! Spread the news, and hurry!"

Talia hoped her explanation would suffice. In the knowledge that they had to act fast, that's all she had to offer. The Sprightlys would soon be arriving in full force.

"They're here," shouted Mrs Gould. "Use your magic, Talia. Remember to focus your energy. Feel the power running through your body and towards your fingertips. Strike the enemy with intent."

Entering the area of sky directly above Talia, was a determined Sprightly, his malicious intent clear in the fiery orb he conjured in his hand. Reacting on pure instinct, Talia swiftly manoeuvred to evade the impending danger, narrowly dodging the searing projectile.

Infuriated by the audacity of the attack, she

then channelled her anger into a retaliatory burst of magic. With fierce determination, she conjured her own orb of fire, unleashing it with precision towards her assailant. The air crackled with energy as the blazing sphere streaked through the sky, finding its mark with unerring accuracy.

A pained cry ripped through the air as the Sprightly's form became engulfed by the flames, his wings faltering as he struggled to maintain control. Talia watched with grim satisfaction as her adversary's movements grew erratic, his once-confident demeanour now giving way to desperation in the face of her counterattack.

"Leave Calyun at once," she commanded. "You'll regret it if you don't."

To her amazement, the wounded Sprightly flew up higher into the air, his compromised wings beating weakly, but frantically, as he disappeared out of sight, his retreat a testament to the potency of Talia's defence.

My magic must have really hurt him.

Despite the slight pang of guilt tugging at her

conscience, Talia knew that her actions had been driven by necessity. The safety of her village hung in the balance, and she couldn't afford to hesitate in defending it against the impending threat. Besides, although one enemy had been repelled, she knew that the battle was far from over. There was no telling when or where the next assault would come from.

"Watch out, Talia!" Mrs Gould shouted, urgency echoing in her voice.

As she whirled around in disbelief, Talia's senses jolted to high alert when she registered the flames being hurled at her by another Sprightly. She instinctively recoiled, her body lurching backwards in a bid to dodge the blazing onslaught.

"I'm ok," she yelled, keen to reassure her ally.

Mrs Gould nodded confidently and charged towards another Sprightly, their movements dominating the azure expanse. With lightning-fast reflexes, the foe attempted to tear at her wings from behind. Mrs Gould somersaulted and forcefully kicked her legs out at him. The impact caused the Sprightly to plummet towards the ground to be captured by the villagers, who still seemed more bewildered than decisive in their actions.

Like a bird of prey, Mrs Gould then charged at another Sprightly. Caught by surprise, he soon tumbled out of the air and down towards the cobblestones to be outnumbered by the frantic crowd growing hungry for justice.

"That's all of them," she called out to Talia. "Everyone has either retreated or been captured."

Talia gazed down at the villagers, most of whom were still gripping weapons in their hands. Despite how they had already doused the few fires ignited by the Sprightlys, it was evident that everyone was still tense.

"Listen," Talia called down to the crowd. "We're on your side. We're going to land now. Stand back!"

Too dazed to do anything other than comply with the instruction, the villagers backed away, allowing Talia and Mrs Gould to land safely in the village square.

"You don't need to fear magic!" Talia said. "Magic is only a threat when it's being used by fae with bad intent. There's no such thing as bad magic, just bad fae."

"Talia?" a familiar male voice called out from the crowd.

"Father," she said, emotion in her voice as she spotted him standing next to her mother. "I've missed you both so much."

"Talia, we've missed you dearly," her mother said, her eyes glistening with tears.

"You're glowing with magic," her father said gruffly.

"Calyun was under attack by the Sprightlys," Talia explained firmly. "*They* are the enemy – not the magic itself. *We* used magic to send them away."

"Hmm..." her father mused.

Sarelda turned her attention towards Mrs Gould. The teacher noticed, and humbly took a tentative step forward.

"Hello," she said, addressing Talia's mother with respect. "I'm one of the teachers at Rosethorn Academy. I want to make it clear that we do not condone violence, but when Talia told me that the Sprightlys were heading towards her village, I couldn't stand by and let it be destroyed."

"Thank you so much," Sarelda whispered, her tone full of gratitude and relief.

"There's a whole world of magic out there, Mother," said Talia. "It is only as good and as helpful as the intent of the fae wishing to use it. I hope that now you've seen what it can do, that you – and anyone else who may fear it – will be able to appreciate it for what it truly is."

Sarelda took a step back before exchanging a thoughtful glance with her husband, who nodded back at her in agreement.

"I'm sorry for doubting you, Talia," she said. "And I'm sorry that we doubted magic, and Rosethorn Academy. You only want to do what's right. We can see that now."

"I promise to come back and visit," Talia said.

"I will be keeping a very close eye on Calyun from now on. The Sprightlys had better steer clear of it."

"Well," said Mrs Gould. "I'm not sure that we should be in a hurry to go into battle again. That said, I am incredibly proud of you, Talia. When we get back to the academy, I shall need to discuss future plans with Professor Thistle."

Talia nodded understandingly. She couldn't ignore the fact that Mrs Gould had taken a significant risk; she had gone against what was expected of her as a representative of Rosethorn Academy and its teachings.

"Thank you, Talia," said her father.

"You're welcome," she said, appreciative of his approval. "We had better head back."

"Indeed," said Mrs Gould. "The magic will wear off soon and we've got just enough power left for the flight back to Priggly."

"Be careful out there," said Sarelda.

"I will," said Talia, relieved that she had

reconnected with her parents, and calm in the knowledge that they were no longer in danger.

With a sparkle in her eyes, she smiled at her parents and then looked over to Mrs Gould, who nodded to signal that it was time to go. With the power of the rose thorn magic still surging through them, they jumped up into the air for the flight back.

Epilogue

As soon as Talia got back to the academy from Calyun, she went straight up to her room, secluding herself there for three days straight. During that time, Perin, Beagan and Heather regularly stopped by to visit and deliver her meals. Although she proudly stood by her decision to defend her village, Talia knew that she couldn't underestimate what the reaction may be from not only Professor Thistle, but from other students and teachers too. There was also a part of her that feared Mrs Gould would be in trouble. She hated to think that the wonderful teacher's career could be at stake. Mrs Gould had, after all, put some of her deepest beliefs on the line in order to help protect Calyun from the Sprightlys.

Upon first hearing of what had happened in

Calyun, Professor Thistle was deeply upset. It angered him to know that everything about Rosethorn Academy's values had been disregarded by not only a student, but a teacher as well. Although he'd had a clear idea that Talia was interested in fighting to stop the Sprightlys, he had been holding on to the hope that her ideas would change as she progressed through her studies.

Luckily for Talia, and indeed Mrs Gould, the professor quickly rejected his thoughts on asking anyone to leave the academy, for within days, he received many letters from Calyun and beyond. In each of them, fae expressed their gratitude and admiration for what Talia and Mrs Gould had done, often stating that they were a credit to the academy. Following this turn of events, Professor Thistle held a series of consultations with several stakeholders. They all agreed that going forward, the best approach – albeit as a last resort – would be to use magic for defence. No longer would the academy keep a low profile when any town or village was under attack.

Throughout her three-year stay at Rosethorn Academy, Talia embraced her studies, expanding her knowledge of plant magic and how to use it to its full potential. With the support of Mrs Gould and other experts, she mastered not only the magic of rose thorns, but of many other plants too. Having first used rose thorn magic to protect Calyun, and highly aware that such power should never be underestimated, she was happy to take a step back to focus on the basics.

With the academy embracing a new approach in how to deal with the Sprightlys, a range of new classes were added to the curriculum. Along with every other student, Talia studied the morals and ethics of how to use magic for good in a way that was active rather than passive. As had been the case with the previous curriculum, the wellbeing of faekind remained paramount and was always at the heart of everything.

After completing her studies at Rosethorn Academy, Talia kept in touch with everyone. She would occasionally drop by to help Heather in the kitchen – for old times' sake, and to have a good catch-up. The two of them were always pleased to do some baking together.

For the years that followed, Talia made it her mission to educate others about magic. She travelled to the many towns and villages around the academy and beyond, keen to tell them about how magic was there to help them, and of how if they ever needed assistance, they had only to ask. For of course, Talia's initial battle with the Sprightlys was just the first of many for her. With bad fae always willing to use magic for evil, the need to stay vigilant would always remain.

Due to her time at Rosethorn Academy, Talia knew deep in her heart that the power of plant magic would be with her for life, and for good.

www.ingramcontent.com/pod-product-compliance
Lightning Source LLC
Chambersburg PA
CBHW061454210726
48287CB00007B/2509